Please return/renew this item by the last date shown
on this label, or on your self-service receipt.

To renew this item, visit **www.librarieswest.org.uk**
or contact your library.

Your Borrower Number and PIN are required.

Libraries West

HENRY POND
the Poet

HENRY POND
the Poet

Dick King-Smith

With illustrations by
Victor Ambrus

Barrington Stoke

First published in 2017 in Great Britain by
Barrington Stoke Ltd
18 Walker Street, Edinburgh, EH3 7LP

www.barringtonstoke.co.uk

Text © 1989 Fox Busters Ltd
Illustrations © 2017 Victor Ambrus

A CIP catalogue record for this book is available
from the British Library upon request

ISBN: 978-1-78112-590-8

Printed in China by Leo

This book is super readable for young readers beginning their
independent reading journey

Contents

Chapter 1
Pride of the Toads

Henry Pond was a poet. All the other toads in the neighbourhood were very proud of this fact. When they spoke of him they never referred to him as just "Henry Pond", much less plain old "Henry". They always called him "Henry Pond the Poet".

Toads take their family names from their places of birth, the water in which they hatched from spawn to tadpole. "River" is a common surname for toads, as are "Lake" and "Pool". There are a few families who affect double-barrelled names such as "Mill-Pool" or "Duck-Pond". "Pond" is probably the commonest surname of all, but everyone agreed that Henry's gift for poetry was most uncommon.

Everyone croaked whenever Henry's name was mentioned. They never missed a chance to mention it at the top of their voices in front of such lesser creatures as frogs and newts.

Two toads might be sitting side by side, saying nothing, staring vacantly out of their bulgy golden eyes, when a frog would chance to hop past.

Right away the two toads would start a loud conversation between themselves.

"Forgot to tell you," one might say. "Met Henry Pond the Poet yesterday."

"Not Henry Pond the Poet?" the other would ask.

"Yes. What a talented toad, eh?"

"Indeed he is. Sure to win first prize at the Eis-TOAD-fod," the first toad would boast.

"Makes you proud to be one of us, what?"

And then the frog would say, in a tone of amazement, "A poet? A toad that makes up poems?"

And the toads would reply, "Hop it, Frog Face. We weren't croaking to you."

And then they would sit in happy silence again, waiting for another passer-by and another chance to sing the praises of Henry Pond the Poet.

Chapter 2
Henry

Even as a tiny tadpole, Henry's talents had been clear. His very first poem showed this. It went –

Oh, how I long and long for legs,
   First two, and later, more
For it is sure as eggs is eggs
   I'll finish up with four.

And I shall give three rousing cheers
  To see my tail grow shorter,
Till TOADally it disappears
  And I can leave the water.

  Henry would recite this poem to all his thousands of fellow tadpoles – or TOADpoles, as he called them in his poetic way – as they swam about the pond together.

But ducks, newts, fish and water-beetles all gobbled up the little TOADpoles, and day by day fewer ... and fewer ... TOADpoles of the Pond family were left to listen to the poem.

At the two-legged stage, there were hundreds to hear it. At the four-legged stage, dozens only. By the time their tails had disappeared and they were ready to emerge from the water as toadlets, only a handful remained to hear the latest work of Henry Pond the Poet.

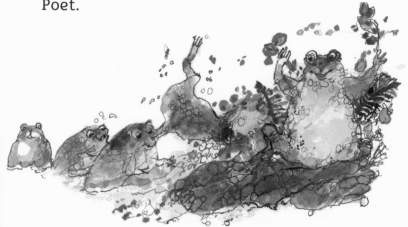

Remember now our friends of yore

That vanished down the fish's maw,

Or in the water-beetle's jaw,

Or duck's webbed paw, or newt's sharp

claw.

Though they have passed through Death's

dark door,

They are not lost, but gone before.

The survivors thought this a very beautiful poem, and a sly tear dropped from many a golden eye.

Before long, however, many a golden eye closed, never to re-open. This was because its owner had not listened carefully enough to the next poem by Henry Pond the Poet –

Now, never speak to strangers –

   A crow, a snake, a rat –

For life is full of dangers,

   And cows will squash you flat.

And flatly you'll be sorry

   If you should cross the road –

It doesn't take a lorry

   To pulverise a toad.

Chapter 3
Fame

Not all of Henry's poems were gloomy. As he grew to toad's estate and put away tadpole-ish things, he began to explore the pleasures of grown-up life, and a good deal of his poetry was full of joy.

It was at this stage that the other toad families – the Rivers, the Lakes, the Pools and the others – began to speak of Henry for the first time as Henry Pond the Poet. By now Henry was living in an old stone shed. It was a splendid pad, dark, damp and snail-filled, and Henry shared it with several other young bachelor toads. It was here that he began his poetry readings.

Every month, at the time of the full moon, a large company of local toads would gather to hear the poet croak his latest piece and to enjoy many of the old favourites.

Poems about food were always popular.

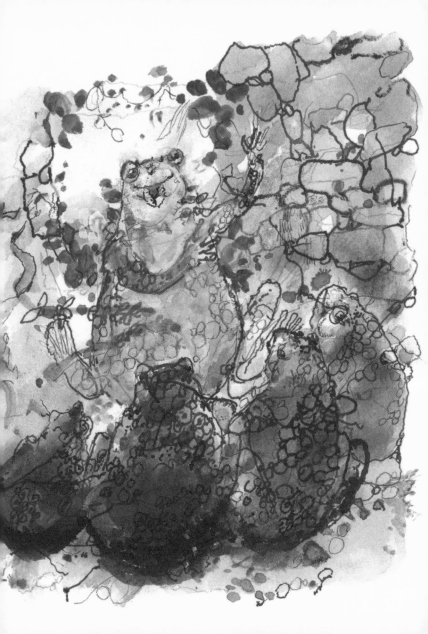

Oh, worms are nice and slugs are nice
And the centipedes and the old woodlice,
But search as you may o'er hill and dale,
There's nothing as nice as a big fat snail.

Each verse was followed by a rousing chorus. To appreciate this one, you must realise that every toad can draw its eyes down into its head, and squash its prey between the bottom of the eyeballs and the tongue.

Fee fi fo fung!

    Squeeze your eyeballs on your tongue!

Fung fo fi fee!

    Squash a slimy snail for tea!

Beetles are nice and bugs are nice

    And a litter of wriggling baby mice,

But search as you may o'er dale and hill,

    A big fat snail's the nicest still.

To begin with, Henry would recite this poem alone, but the other toads soon learned the words of the chorus. Each time the poet finished a verse, the whole crowd would croak together –

"Fee fi fo fung!

Squeeze your eyeballs on your tongue!

Fung fo fi fee!

Squash a slimy snail for tea!"

It was at one of these full-moon recitals, just as the sound of that chorus died away, that Henry Pond the Poet fell in love.

Chapter 4
In Love

The girl was squatting in the front row. Her mouth was open, her golden eyes were fixed upon Henry. She was hypnotised, it seemed, by his poetry.

Henry delivered his final set of verses. Then, as the crowd began to crawl away, he waddled over to consult one of his friends.

"Who is that amazing, lovely girl in the front row?" he whispered.

"Oh, that's Victoria Garden-Pool," his friend said. "Tadpole of her year, she was, and many consider her a great beauty now she's fully grown."

With fast-beating heart, Henry approached the great beauty. She was covered, he could see, with the most delightful thick warts. Her eyes were half closed now and her mouth hung wider still. Henry supposed her to be overcome at his recital. He was about to speak, when suddenly she yawned, opened her eyes and said, "Is it finished?"

"Yes," Henry said. "Did you enjoy it?"

"Enjoy it?" Victoria Garden-Pool croaked. "I have seldom spent such a boring evening. Who on earth was that toad spouting all that rubbish?"

Henry opened his mouth to say "Me".
Then he realised that Victoria did not
recognise him and instead he replied,
"That was Henry Pond the Poet."

"He seems very fond of the sound of his own voice," Victoria Garden-Pool said. "Poets are all the same, I suppose – wet and windy like the weather. Myself, I prefer toads of action." And with that, she turned her warty back on Henry and waddled out.

"Wait!" Henry called, and crawled after her. But when he got outside he could see that there was a toad waiting

for Victoria – a burly muscular fellow
who looked very much a toad of action.

Henry waddled over to his friend
again.

"Who's that?" he said.

"That," his friend said, "is Larry Lake.
They say that when he was a tadpole,
he fought off a minnow. And he's been

known to eat a full-grown mouse, tail and all. He's crawling out with Victoria. I shouldn't tangle with him, if I were you."

"Oh," said Henry Pond the Poet. "Oh dear."

And Henry Pond the Poet watched sadly as Victoria Garden-Pool and Larry Lake disappeared into the night.

Chapter 5
Tough

In the weeks that followed, as the moon waned and waxed again, Henry could think of only one thing. Would Victoria come to his next poetry reading?

It didn't seem likely, but maybe Larry Lake would bring her – if he was fond of poetry, but that didn't seem likely either.

Just in case, Henry worked hard on a new poem. It was a love poem. He would pour out his heart as he squatted before Victoria, gazing into her eyes, croaking to her and her alone. He finished it just before the moon was full again.

Come swim with me and be my love –

    The fish below, the birds above –

Come swim with me from shore to shore

    And be my love for ever more!

Come hop with me across the vale,

    We'll feast on worm and slug and snail!

Come, fairest toad I ever saw,

    And be my love for ever more!

Come crawl with me along the strand,

Sit by the water, hand in hand,

And dream of joys that lie in store

And be my love for ever more!

But, alas! When the crowd gathered once again to hear the latest works of Henry Pond the Poet, Victoria Garden-Pool was not among them.

Henry did not feel he could recite his new love poem. It was for Victoria and Victoria only. But in case she did not come he had prepared another new poem of quite a different type.

Ever since Victoria had declared her liking for toads of action, Henry had been trying hard to convince himself that he was one.

He practised blowing himself up to look large and terrifying, and he practised making clumsy hops at invisible enemies.

'You may fancy yourself as a real He-Toad, Larry Lake,' he said to himself, 'but Henry Pond is not just a poet, you know. He too is a toad of action!'

Henry's new poem was designed to let his listeners know this –

Who is bold and strong and rough?
  Shout it out! You know it!
Who is brave and fierce and tough?

And then, Henry thought, the crowd would all say –

Henry Pond the Poet!

But that evening things did not turn out as Henry Pond had hoped. Once he had seen that Victoria Garden-Pool was not present, he tried out the second of his two new poems.

He said –

Who is bold and strong and rough?

Shout it out! You know it!

Who is brave and fierce and tough?

And a voice at the back croaked –

Larry Lake!

Chapter 6
Stupid Toad

"No, no!" Henry snapped. "You should have said 'Henry Pond the Poet'. 'Poet' rhymes with 'know it'. 'Larry Lake' doesn't rhyme with anything. Who was the stupid toad who said that?"

At this, there was a stir in the audience. A burly muscular toad was bullocking his way past the others. He shouldered several toads out of his path until at last he squatted face to face with Henry.

"I was that stupid toad," Larry Lake said.

"Oh," said Henry Pond the Poet. "Oh dear."

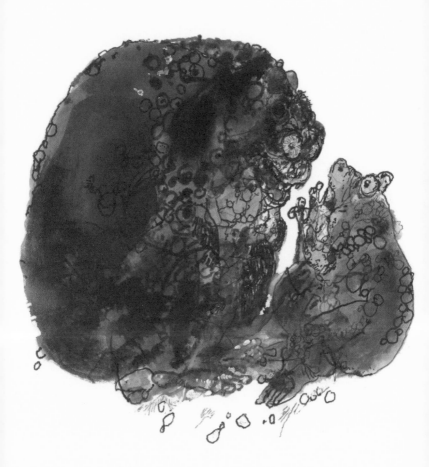

"And since you're so rough and tough," Larry said, "come on outside."

As you know, toads are cold-blooded creatures, but Henry's blood ran even colder now. "What for?" he said.

"That's what I'm going to give you," said Larry Lake. "I'm going to give you what for. I saw you making eyes at my lady friend, don't think I didn't. Now I'm going to give you a good hiding."

For a moment the crowd was silent, stunned by this sudden drama in the midst of a reading. Then they began to realise that a wrestling match might be a nice change from poetry. They started to move out as one, carrying Henry and Larry along with them.

Outside, they formed a ring round the two toads.

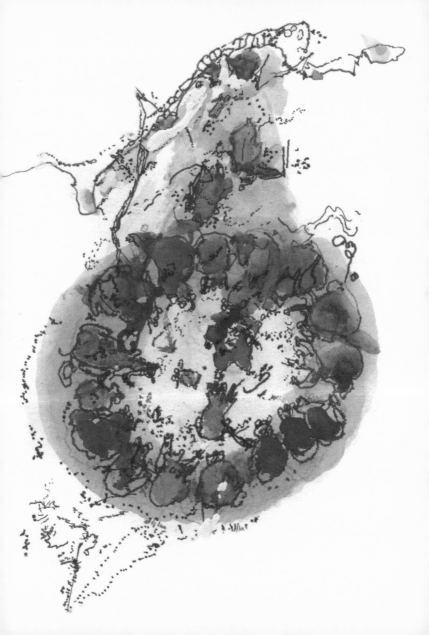

There were a few who began to root for Larry – some of the Lake family and some who wanted to toady to Larry. They cheered him with croaks of, "Get him, Larry boy! Squeeze his eyeballs on his tongue!"

But Larry's bully-boy ways had not made him popular and there were many who were cheering for Henry.

"Who is bold and strong and rough?
    Hear us shout! We know it!
Who is brave and fierce and tough?
    Henry Pond the Poet!"

Then silence fell as an old and respected toad entered the ring to act as referee.

"You know the rules," he said to the contestants. "Three falls or two submissions. And may the best toad win!"

Chapter 7
Victory

Henry sat very still, and wished very much that he had not made up such a silly poem. He had never enjoyed rough games, and he had no idea what to do. But Larry Lake had. He crawled forward, got behind Henry, and wrapped his forearms around the poet's neck.

Then, with one almighty heave, he pulled Henry over onto his back.

Henry lay kicking helplessly, while the referee called above the noise of the crowd, "Fall number one!"

Larry Lake sat and waited for Henry to right himself. 'I wish the Garden-Pool girl was here,' he thought, 'to see me make a mess of this wimp ...' – and at that moment he spotted her. She was crawling up to the ringside, attracted by all the noise.

"Hi, Victoria!" Larry croaked. "Watch this! A big Lake beats a little Pond any day!"

The sound of his beloved's name made Henry turn his head to look at her. As he did so, Larry Lake took a large hop forward … and butted him under the chin.

Once again Henry fell flat on his back.

"Fall number two!" the referee called.

The Lake supporters were jubilant! One more fall and the match was Larry's.

"Easy! Easy!" they began to chant, while Henry's fans were silent and gloomy as their toad struggled to his feet once more.

They waited for what seemed the certain end to the fight.

Larry Lake waited, his face split in a sneering grin.

Victoria Garden-Pool waited, her golden eyes fixed upon the toad of action.

"Come on, Larry!" she called. She did not spare a glance for the poet.

Henry waited too, for his head to clear. When at last it did, he found, rather to his surprise, that he was very angry.

'Who is brave and fierce and tough?'
he asked himself. 'Why, I am!'

And he crawled swiftly towards
Larry Lake, shot out his large flat pink
sticky tongue and hit his opponent in the
eye.

As Larry reeled, half-blinded, Henry
hit him in the other eye.

Then he grabbed one of Larry's long hind legs and began to bend it the wrong way. He bent harder and harder, until at last the toad of action beat on the ground with his front foot in a token of defeat.

"Submission number one!" the referee called.

Henry was a good sport and waited until Larry had cleaned his eyes. But for all he was still, his mind was racing.

'I mustn't let him close with me,' he thought. 'He's much stronger and heavier. But he's slow. I must keep out of his way, wear him down, tire him out.'

And that is exactly what happened. Henry side-stepped every leap and lunge that Larry made. He ducked under every hop, and slipped out from every grasp. At last the big toad sat – worn out, puffing and blowing in the middle of the ring.

Then Henry heard a single voice above the noise of the crowd, a voice that was heavenly music in his ears.

"Come on, Henry!" Victoria Garden-Pool called. At that, Henry leaped upon his enemy's broad back and got him in a full nelson. He pressed down with super-toadish strength until at last, in a strangled broken croak, Larry Lake cried, "I submit, I submit!"

The referee hopped forward and raised the front foot of Henry Pond the Poet high in victory.

Chapter 8
Moonlight

Much later that night, Henry and
Victoria sat by the water, hand in hand.
The words of the poet floated out over
the moonlit ripples –

Come swim with me and be my love –

    The fish below, the birds above –

Come swim with me from shore to shore

    And be my love for ever more!

Come hop with me across the vale,

    We'll feast on worm and slug and snail!

Come fairest toad I ever saw

    And be my love for ever more!

Come crawl with me along the strand,

    Sit by the water, hand in hand,

And dream of joys that lie in store,

And be my love for ever more!

"It's funny," Victoria said. "When I first heard your poetry, I didn't think much of it. But I do like that one. Am I really the fairest toad you ever saw, Henry?"

"You are," said Henry.

"In that case," said Victoria, "I think I should rather like to be your love for ever more."

And then she heard the shortest of all Henry's many compositions.

"Oh Victoria!

I adore ya!"

said Henry Pond the Poet.

The RATS
of Meadowsweet Farm

Little Gems

Dick King-Smith

Illustrations by Victor Ambrus

Baby rats
Buck rats
And a King Rat ...

Meadowsweet Farm is running with rats, thanks to Farmer Green and his grotty ways. Farmer Green wants rid of the rats, and Ripper the King Rat wants rid of Farmer Green.

Who will win the war?